I had a big bear who will always be with me.
This book is for all the bears like him.
Margarita del Mazo

To Dad and Charlie, my two bears.
Rocio Bonilla

My Big Bear, My Little Bear and Me
Somos8 Series

© Text: Margarita del Mazo, 2018
© Illustrations: Rocio Bonilla, 2018
© Edition: NubeOcho, 2019
www.nubeocho.com · hello@nubeocho.com

Original title: *Mi oso grande, mi oso pequeño y yo*
English translation: Ben Dawlatly
Text editing: Rebecca Packard

Distributed in the United States by
Consortium Book Sales & Distribution

First edition: 2019
ISBN: 978-84-17123-50-5

Printed in China by Asia Pacific Offset,
respecting international labor standards.

MY BIG
BEAR
MY LITTLE BEAR
AND ME

MARGARITA DEL MAZO   ROCIO BONILLA

nubeOCHO

It's good to have a bear.
But I have two, and that's better.

I take them with me everywhere.

The big one is as strong as a giant
and lets me see the world from up high.

The little one is soft like cotton
and brings me close to the tiny things.

The big one protects me
from the cold.

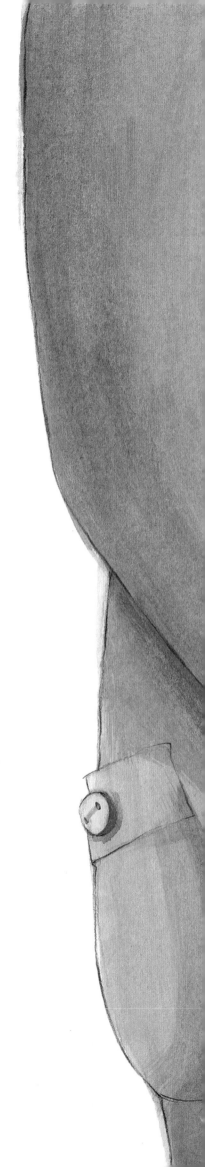

He always shows me surprising things.

The little one helps me to make friends…

...loads of friends.

My bears never leave me
when things get tough.

When I'm very tired, they
encourage me to carry on.

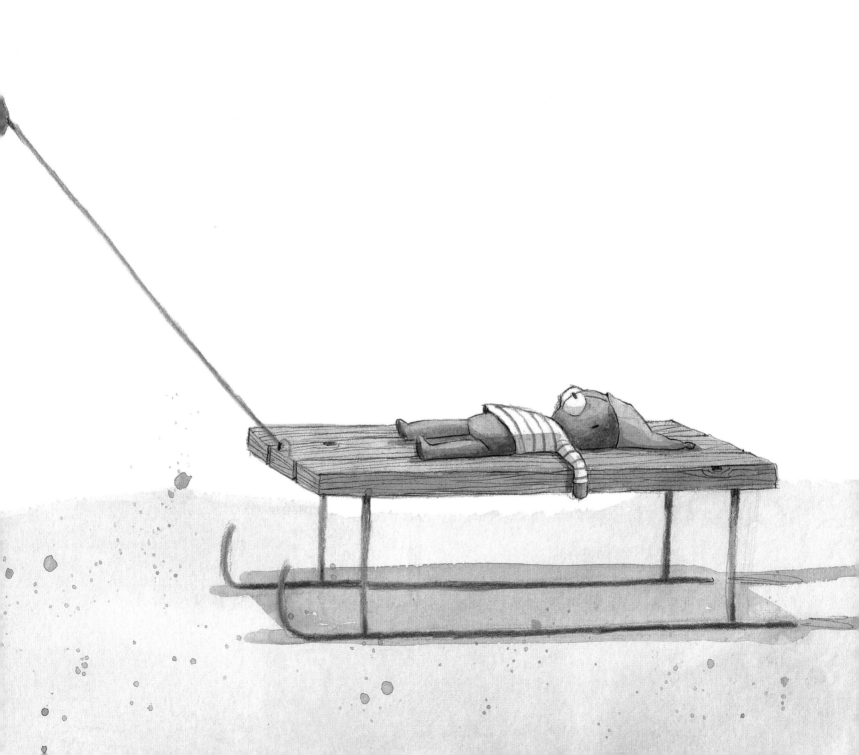

If you have a big bear and a little bear,
you'll never lose your way.

I know that my little bear needs me.

And sometimes my big bear too.

It's good to have a bear.
But I have two,
and that's much better.